SUPERPOWER SISTERHOOD

JENNA BUSH HAGER &
BARBARA PIERCE BUSH

ILLUSTRATED BY CYNDI WOJCIECHOWSKI

Little, Brown and Company
New York • Boston

Welcome to Humble Street, population 38.

I've lived here my whole life. Just me, Mom and Dad, and our closest neighbors: the Millers, the Díazes, the Franks, and the Rosas.

I've gotten really good at only-kid-on-the-block stuff:

I perform puppet shows for my fish, Mr. Hooter.

Mom and Dad and I have Friday night dance parties.

And I conquer the math-team championship every year!

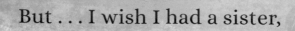
But . . . I wish I had a sister,

or a neighbor my own age.

(Someone to walk with me past that witchy Ms. Wigglestoot in house #13.)

After months of wishing on stars . . .
it finally happened!

Two houses down,
a moving van full of
instruments and books
rolled in, and out
popped Lila and Liliani.

Across the street, a truck packed with tools and costumes drove up, and Danielle and Didi (and their poodle, PomPom) danced out into the road!

"Go introduce yourself," my mama said as I peeked at the sisters through our front door.

Mama was right. This was what I'd been wishing for: some friends!

"Hi, I'm Emma . . . the resident expert around here! I want to offer you my touring, exploring, and introducing services."

And, just like that, we were off: playing
hide-and-seek in the honeysuckle field
behind the Franks' house,

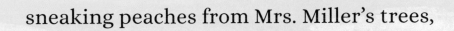
sneaking peaches from Mrs. Miller's trees,

and skateboarding as fast as we
could past evil Ms. Wigglestoot's house.
I'd found my friends—my sisters!

The sisters and I (an honorary sister!) began daily meetings of the Humble Street Sisterhood.

"We need a place to call our own," I said.

"Let's build a *she* shed!" said Danielle,
pulling out her pencils.

Danielle's design was the best thing she'd ever drawn!

I made sure the math worked out—all in my head!

Lila's song to pass the time had the birds singing along.

Did our sisterhood have . . . superpowers?

"Let's take these talents to the street," I declared.

Danielle and I worked to fix Mr. Potty's potty

and built planters for Mrs. Rosa's roses.

Didi the dancer choreographed an epic flash mob, "The Sister Shuffle," that the Smiths and the Franks couldn't resist.

Liliani wrote a limerick that
made the whole block laugh.

But even Lila's sweetest song couldn't get *everyone* outside.

Yup, it seemed that when we were together,
our sisterhood could do almost anything.

We each had powers,

HOMES FOR PAWS CONCERT

CONCERT FOR the Animal Rescue Center

but together
they were SUPER.

To record our magic, Liliani brought her grandmother's old diary to our shed. I turned the crackly, empty pages and wrote:

With these powers, we will do good deeds, nurture nature, uplift others, and above all else, support our sisterhood! Sissy Power, unite!

A few days later, as we chanted our oath, PomPom barked! A dark shadow passed by the front of our shed—and our super-secret diary was gone!

"That spooky Ms. Wigglestoot must be spying on our powers!" I said.

"I bet she stole our diary!" Liliani added.

We decided to spy right back to figure out where our diary was hidden.

Lila composed a warning song—alerting us when danger was near.

Danielle disguised our she shed.

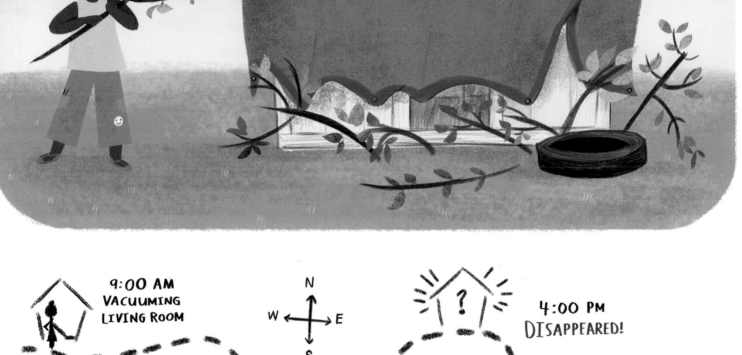

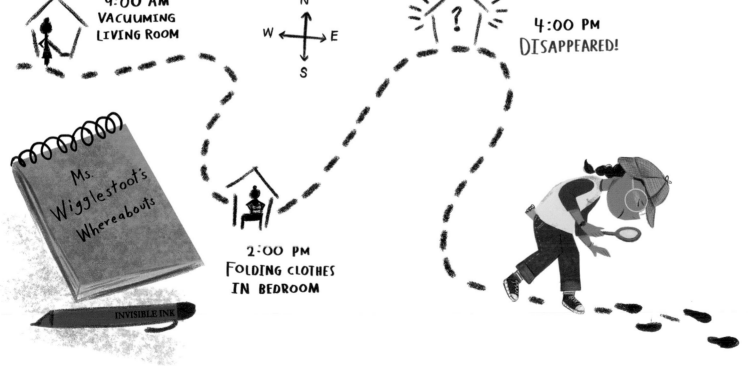

9:00 AM
VACUUMING
LIVING ROOM

N
W ← → E
S

4:00 PM
DISAPPEARED!

Ms. Wigglestoot's Whereabouts

INVISIBLE INK

2:00 PM
FOLDING CLOTHES
IN BEDROOM

And I mapped out Ms. Wigglestoot's daily route.

We were vigilant. We spied her reading (a book of spells, obviously) and cooking (probably a rat for her dinner).

But . . . well . . . then things got boring. Ms. Wigglestoot
wasn't doing much.

It was time to steal our super-secret diary back.

All of a sudden, it was code red!
Ms. Wigglestoot was walking right
toward us—with our diary under her arm!

"Hi, Emma," she said, in a much nicer voice than I'd expected. "This fell out of your backpack when you ran past my house the other day. I hope you don't mind my reading it . . . and adding a little something of my own."

"Um . . . thank you," I said, then dashed back to our shed with my sisters.

"What did she write?" Didi asked.

I flipped through the pages until I saw something new on the last one:

Dear Sisters,

I never had anyone to share my secrets with or to help me build a clubhouse, but I've admired you from afar. Your sisterhood empowers! Watching you make this street a better, kinder place with your magnificent talents has made me feel young again.

Wilma Wigglestoot

And the next day, we knew what we had to do.

"With these powers, I will do good deeds . . ."

"Superpower sisters, unite!"

To our daughters—
may you use your powers to empower others.
—JBH & BPB

To my sister, Ann.
—CW

ABOUT THIS BOOK

The illustrations for this book were done in Adobe Photoshop and Illustrator. This book was edited by Deirdre Jones and designed by Angelie Yap with art direction by Saho Fujii. The production was supervised by Virginia Lawther, and the production editor was Jen Graham. The text was set in Alice Std, and the display type is Colby Condensed.

Text and illustrations copyright © 2022 by Jenna Bush Hager and Barbara Pierce Bush • Illustrations by Cyndi Wojciechowski • Cover illustration by Cyndi Wojciechowski • Cover design by Angelie Yap • Cover copyright © 2022 by Hachette Book Group, Inc. • Hachette Book Group supports the right to free expression and the value of copyright. The purpose of copyright is to encourage writers and artists to produce the creative works that enrich our culture. • The scanning, uploading, and distribution of this book without permission is a theft of the author's intellectual property. If you would like permission to use material from the book (other than for review purposes), please contact permissions@hbgusa.com. Thank you for your support of the author's rights. • Little, Brown and Company • Hachette Book Group • 1290 Avenue of the Americas, New York, NY 10104 • Visit us at LBYR.com • First Edition: April 2022 • Little, Brown and Company is a division of Hachette Book Group, Inc. • The Little, Brown name and logo are trademarks of Hachette Book Group, Inc. • The publisher is not responsible for websites (or their content) that are not owned by the publisher. • Library of Congress Cataloging-in-Publication Data • Names: Hager, Jenna Bush, 1981– author. | Bush, Barbara, 1981– author. | Wojciechowski, Cyndi, illustrator. • Title: The superpower sisterhood / Jenna Bush Hager, Barbara Pierce Bush ; illustrated by Cyndi Wojciechowski. • Description: First edition. | New York : Little, Brown and Company, 2022. | Audience: Ages 4–8 | Summary: When two sets of sisters move into Emma's neighborhood, they all form a club celebrating their individual talents, which turn out to be almost superhero-like when the girls work together. • Identifiers: LCCN 2021027567 | ISBN 9780316628440 (hardcover) | ISBN 9780759554429 (ebook) • Subjects: CYAC: Friendship—Fiction. | Sisters—Fiction. | Cooperativeness—Fiction. • Classification: LCC PZ7.1.H233 Su 2022 | DDC [E]—dc23 • LC record available at https://lccn.loc.gov/2021027567 • ISBNs: 978-0-316-62844-0 (hardcover), 978-0-7595-5442-9 (ebook), 978-0-7595-5443-6 (ebook), 978-0-7595-5441-2 (ebook) • PRINTED IN THE UNITED STATES OF AMERICA • PHX • 10 9 8 7 6 5 4 3 2 1

As young girls, we often threw our fists in the air, mimicking superheroes, and in unison squealed, "Twin Powers, unite!" In our imaginations, there was nothing we couldn't do with our sister by our side.

Our mom is an only child, and Emma is very much inspired by her. Our mother's friends were her sisters, and they each brought their gifts—love of poetry, art, design, reading, and math. Separately, they were super; together they were super powerful!

That same camaraderie and fearlessness has accompanied us as we've grown older. And it's increased as our crew of "sisters" has expanded to include friends and colleagues—women who celebrate our unique abilities and encourage us to use them.

The Superpower Sisterhood is a love letter to all women and girls, a reminder that the power of sisterhood can, and should, provide us with the confidence to be the most brave, unique, and loving versions of ourselves.

Art Auction for Children's Hospital

Monarch Butterfly Garden

Lemonade for Clean Water

Senior Spring Dance

Beach Cleanup